One
Dropped Key

can lead to so much more

a steamy roommates short story

K.E. Monteith

ONE DROPPED KEY

A steamy roommates short story

K.E. Monteith

CONTENTS

Title Page

Copyright

Author's Note

Dedication

Chapter 1   1

Chapter 2   6

Chapter 3   12

Chapter 4   18

Chapter 5   23

Chapter 6   31

Chapter 7   37

Chapter 8   43

Chapter 9   49

Chapter 10   54

Chapter 11   61

Epilogue   69

About the author   73

Books By This Author   75

Upcoming release   77

Preview of Quitting My Boss   79

AUTHOR'S NOTE

Please note that this short story contains sexually explicit scenes that are not appropriate for children.

Here for a fun time, not a long time

CHAPTER 1

Kasey

It should be acknowledged that my current situation is entirely my fault. You don't just agree to let a man live in your guest room for an indeterminate amount of time. It doesn't matter that he's a good friend of your good friend. It doesn't matter that he's just in-between places and the housing market is crap. It doesn't matter that when you met for coffee to test the waters, he bought the drinks. It doesn't matter that when you spilled said coffee all over yourself like an idiot, he didn't make fun of you or gawk at your now see-through shirt. And it most certainly didn't matter how attracted you are to him, even if your only intentions are having someone nice to look at around the house. You will either start getting attached or annoyed about sharing your living after several years of living alone. Or in my case, both.

"Kasey, I know you're particular about your peanut butter brand, but JIF's been out of stock for, like, months now. So will you kill me if I just go ahead and buy Skippy?" Matt asked, facing the wall of peanut butter. The harsh fluorescent lights did nothing to diminish the charming smile he shot me. Rude.

"No."

"No, you won't kill me or no, don't get the Skippy?"

I sighed. "Both."

"So, we just can't have any peanut butter in the house?" Despite his teasing tone, Matt set the Skippy back on the shelf. I had to bite my lip to keep from calling him a good boy.

"We can have peanut butter once JIF's returned. In the meantime, ..."

Matt pushed the cart a step, then paused, staring at me with a raised eyebrow. I bit my lip, trying to think of a way I could maintain my stubborn loyalty to a stupid condiment brand without looking like an asshole.

"I just ... don't like the others," I grumbled.

"Uh-huh. And when exactly was the last time you tried any other brand?" He tilted his body just enough to knock his shoulder against mine. The man had nice arms; how dare he remind me of that fact in the middle of a grocery store on a Friday afternoon.

"Well, this is a JIF household. I won't be jumping ship just because of one little recall."

"Little? It's been months." Right. It had been months since the recall. It'd also been months since he moved into his room. That's right, it didn't even feel like my guest room anymore, it was his. Stupid man stole my room.

"All right, whatever you say, ma'am."

"Don't call me that, we're the same age. And people our age don't need peanut butter anyways." That said, as we passed the Nutella, I grabbed a jar. It was a decent enough substitute for PB&J.

"And the Nutella is for …" It was my turn to nudge his shoulder. And the smile I got in return was well worth any of his little annoyances. Damn it.

"Shut up."

"All right, ma'am." Matt had the audacity to wink as we turned out of the aisle. But before we left, I grabbed some jam. Matt liked to have some with his toast in the morning and he was almost out.

"I should kick you out of my house."

"You wouldn't do that."

I looked over at Matt and tried to get a read on what ludicrous reason he believed was keeping him safe. He'd stayed way past our agreed-upon timeframe. He always left his shoes in the middle of the entryway and I somehow manage to trip over them every damn time, even if they're consistently in the same, albeit wrong, place. And I had been desperately missing my alone time. Alone time to bring someone home so I could forget about him and his well-shaped arms for one damn minute.

But Matt wasn't looking at me, he was looking at the chip display, practically gnawing at his lower lip like he was really considering getting the avocado chips. I'm pretty sure he hates avocados, but maybe he just didn't like the texture.

"You're too nice to kick me out," he finally said, his voice so quiet I almost missed it over the cartwheels rolling by. Maybe that meant he didn't want me to hear him. But I did, so I couldn't *not* reply.

"What do you mean? I'm not that nice."

"You wouldn't have met up with me at all if you weren't."

"I was doing a friend a favor."

"Which is a nice thing to do."

"It's not nice, it's basic decency."

"Mmhmm, and actually letting me stay with you without charging me rent is …" Matt moved on from the chip display and as we passed, I grabbed a bag. Maybe Matt didn't want to admit he wanted to try it, but he stared at them long enough that my curiosity was peaked.

"Because if I ever become homeless, I fully expect you to help me out." The hearty laugh Matt let out drew the attention of all the patrons in the baking aisle. It was admittedly only three people, but I was certain that anyone would be drawn to that laugh. I mean, the way he laughed was free, like nothing else mattered but the moment, like nothing else was dragging down his mind. It was kind of contagious. Or maybe I just wanted it to be. I'd love to have a moment where my mind wasn't buzzing.

"I can't even imagine a scenario where you'd become homeless, Kasey. You're way too put together."

"Put together?" I repeated.

"Yes. You own a home."

"It's a condo. And I'm still paying the mortgage. If I lose my job, I could lose that too."

"Aren't you, like, the only person who knows how

to do half the things at your office?"

"That's irrelevant if the whole company goes out of business."

"Don't be pessimistic, Kas."

I was about to tell him that no one called me Kas, that it gave me flashbacks to an unfortunate Tumblr event, and I'd rather he not call me that. But then as we were turning to the next aisle, his hand went to my waist, guiding me out of the way of oncoming passersby. The touch was so warm, that I almost leaned into it. But I didn't. But only because he moved away too quickly.

Everything was so damn frustrating.

CHAPTER 2

Matt

I think Kasey's getting sick of me. It makes sense. I've been staying at her place, completely rent-free, for almost two months now. It wasn't entirely my fault, finding a place to live has been rough. Everything was either way out of my budget or gone by the time I could fill out an application. Owning or renting.

But also, I wasn't ready to leave. Kasey was fun and smart and so damn sexy in that she won't give you any attention unless you work for it way. And she was especially fun to poke at. She was always so serious and stoic that the one second where her face scrunched up and she tried to figure out what I meant was something I was starting to live for. And the more we got to know each other, the quicker she picked up on when I was joking. Which meant I had to work even harder to get that look of confusion. And honestly, that was the biggest fucking turn own.

Attraction aside, what was even more appealing was that she wasn't afraid to call me out either. When I poke fun at her too much or leave my shoes out or forget to turn off a light. She wasn't afraid of hard, uncomfortable conversations. Or so I had thought. But recently she's been giving me this look, the biting her lip and sucking in her breath look. My best guess is she's working up the nerve to ask me to leave. And I really didn't want that.

So, after we put away the groceries, I snapped my fingers and did my best impression of a man that suddenly remembered something. I could just picture the lightbulb turning on over my head. My performance got a furrowed brow response though, so maybe I went too overboard.

"Sorry, I just remembered that I needed ..." Shit. What did I need? Kasey looked around at the emptied bags, then nodded.

"Toothpaste, right?" How the hell does she do that? She was always noticing what I needed before I did, be it toothpaste, soap, or just a drink. Was that her playing the host? Feeling like she had to look out for me? I didn't want me being here to be work for her. Crap.

"Exactly, toothpaste, right. Gotta have that. I'll probably pick up dinner while I'm out, want anything?" I started towards the door, looking back only when I grabbed my keys off the narrow table in the entryway. Another perfect example of how put together she was. At my old place, I'd never even thought of finding a table like that. If I had, I would've saved at least an hour a month looking for my keys.

"Oh, um, no. I'm good. There's this anime I wanna watch, so I'll probably be in my room for the rest of the night."

"Oh yeah? What's it about?"

She bit her lip and sighed. "This ... spy family."

"That sounds cool, mind if I join you?" I don't normally do cartoons or whatever, but if it meant more time with Kasey before she kicked me out, I was very interested. But she didn't look in the mood. Her eyes were downcast and she kept kicking at a fluff ball on the floor.

"Um, it's in Japanese and I have a hard time concentrating on subtitles with other people around." AKA I'm tired of hanging out with you, Matt, give me my peace and quiet back.

"Understood, no worries."

"It's not ... it's just a me problem. I don't watch foreign shows with anyone else either."

"It's okay, Kasey." I smiled, just to reassure her I wasn't feeling any type of way and tried to tell myself that her considering me a distraction could be a good thing. Lord knows I found her distracting. "If you remember anything else you need from the store or change your mind about food, just text me."

Kasey did the lip thing again before nodding. Ugh, she's definitely gonna kick me out. I wonder how she'll do it. She might give me crap about general roommate shit without qualm, but with something as big as this, she might have a hard time with it. And I really didn't want to make her uncomfortable.

As I walked out of the condo and to my car, I pulled out my phone. And then, as was becoming my newest bad habit, I opened Kasey's first email.

'Dear Matt,

As we discussed, my guest room is available as soon as you need it. I know you insisted on paying some sort of rent, but it's unnecessary. As long as you don't take hour-long showers every day, no compensation is necessary. And I understand you won't have any firm move-out date until you find a place, but again, as long as it's not much longer than a month, I think we can work things out. Just let me know when your ideal move-in date is.

Sincerely,
Kelsey
P.S.
The napkin you wrote your email on got coffee all over it when I knocked over my cup. So, I'm not a hundred percent certain this is your email address. So, if you're receiving this email and have no idea what I'm talking about, please kindly respond to confirm I got the wrong address.'

Was it weird that her short and to-the-point email made me smile?

Fuck the toothpaste, I need a drink.

✽ ✽ ✽

I regretted my decision to go to the bar the minute I parked. But I could see Dylan out on the patio, already waving at me and the text to Kasey that said I'd be out for a couple of hours was already marked as read. So, I had no choice but to follow through.

It's probably a bad sign that I get grumpy when I'm away from Kasey for too long. Probably a sign I should work harder at finding a permanent living situation. But I had the sneaking suspicion that once I moved out, Kasey would never bother interacting with me again. Not in a malicious way, she just tolerated a limited number of social interactions. And unless I did something drastic to make sure she'd miss me, she wasn't going to use that limited energy on me. Too bad my only idea on how to do that was to take her keys.

"Maaaattttt!" someone yelled out my window, quickly followed by loud knocks that had me jumping out of my seat. Hand to heart, I turned to see Dylan had broken the 'no alcohol beyond this point' rule to come over and accost me.

"Fuck off," I groaned, but left the safety of my car anyways.

"What's taking so long?" Dylan wrapped an arm around my shoulder and nearly pulled me towards the bar.

"I was just on my phone ... looking for a place."

Dylan suddenly stopped our walk and slapped my shoulder repeatedly.

"You remember Caleb? He went through some quarter-life crisis thing and quit his job so he can move to Arizona or Nevada or some shit. So, he needs someone to cover his lease!"

"Oh." That was all I could manage as my brain slowly started to parse the information. I'd been to Caleb's place. It was nice, not too expensive, or small. Exactly what I was looking for.

"No, shit, oh. You can finally get out of Kasey's place. You know, have a little freedom, be able to bring a girl home, all that good shit. And I'm sure Kasey will be relieved to have you out of her hair too. I bet you were using all her spoons." And that fact that Dylan could be right was the only reason I immediately headed for Caleb when I got to the bar.

CHAPTER 3

Kasey

"Fuck, yes, yes. Wait, no, no, no, no, no." God mother fucking damn it. So close. I kept getting so close to an orgasm, only to get distracted by thinking about where Matt had gone or move away from the sucker when it was too much, even though that was exactly what I needed. I just needed something else, something to hold me in place and keep me from squirming and drifting.

I turned off the toy and shuffled over to the bedside table. From that, I pulled out headphones and the cuffs. Was it a stupid plan to cuff myself to the headboard? Admittedly, yes. But I was desperate enough to tell Matt he couldn't watch some stupid show with me because being on the couch together would be enough to set me off.

I should talk to him about his moving, I should remind him this wasn't a good permanent solution. But then I start thinking about his stupid shoes and I get frustrated at myself for missing that before he even moved. And that frustration needed to be taken care of before Matt came back. Which meant setting up the friends-to-lovers audio porn playlist, turning up the vibrator, and cuffing myself to the headboard, with the key looped around my fingers and clenched tightly.

I shifted in my bed, turning so that my arms were twisted, elbows rested on my pillow, and I was on my stomach so I could grind into the bed when necessary. I tilted my head to push my headphones against my shoulder and press play.

The audio began slowly. The man was mumbling through an awkward speech about how he never wanted to ruin their friendship but he couldn't ignore how he felt about this girl anymore. And despite my better judgment, I pictured Matt saying those words to me.

"I know you probably don't feel the same way." I do, I think I do. I'm definitely attracted to you, and your stupid arms that stretch over me for the remote when you inevitably say I set the volume too low.

"And I never want to ruin our friendship. So, I think I just … need some time away to get over you." No. I don't want you to go anywhere. I want you to be content staying here, with me.

My thought process seemed to follow the script because as the man was mid-sentence explaining his need for space, he cut off and the sound of kissing followed.

I bet Matt's the kind of kisser that starts off slow. Closed mouth presses of pursed lips. Because he was sweet and if he kissed someone, he wanted it to matter. Matter in a way that was more than just a step towards sex. But he'd succumb to it eventually. Get absorbed by his desire despite himself. And God, do I want that. To kiss him and feel his restraint fall. To have him grip my ass, my hair, whatever he needed to pull me closer, feel me against him. And tease me till I lost control just as badly.

"Are you sure?" Absolutely. "Okay, but … I don't think I'll be able to stop if we keep going." Not a damn problem at all.

The kissing picked up again. Mixed in with sweet little praises I pictured Matt whispering in my ear. "I've dreamed about this for so long and it's still better than I could ever manage."

I think I started imagining things about Matt immediately after our coffee meet-up. It was just those stupid arms. And the not gawking at my wet shirt. And that stupid, dopey smile. And the face he made as he watched me catch on to his jokes.

"Let me get down on my knees for you." Fuck, that's my good boy. He'd look so damn pretty on his knees. And he wouldn't mind if I got distracted or just wanted to keep going because it felt too damn good and I wasn't ready to stop. He'd trace little shapes on my thighs, gripping tightly when I needed it. And he'd ask to keep going. Like he asked to keep watching a show with me last night, even though we both knew he was normally in bed an hour ago. Like he asked to cook every Tuesday and Thursday and even do the dishes after. Like he asked to hang out with me even when I'd been spacing out and not saying anything for hours.

Fuck, I was losing it. I can't think of sweet Matt,

the Matt that was going to leave me one day, probably soon. This was supposed to be a fantasy where Matt lost control and just fucking took me. I didn't need to think about anything more than that.

"So fucking sweet for me. Are you going to come for me? Please?" I pushed my hips down, grinding against the bed in small circles and pushing my clit further into the suction. I hated when a man asked if I was about to come. Even if I was getting close, the question spun my thoughts around. The anxiety of taking too long, the pressure of making them feel inadequate. I'm sure if someone got the timing right, it would be hot. But so far no one had.

"Shit, yes." The sounds of a zipper and rustled clothing brought me back. "Legs around my waist. Yeah, just like that."

What had Matt been doing these past months? He never stayed out late or brought anyone over. Was he laying out in his room, stroking himself? Or did he use the shower? Or had he not done anything at all? Was he just as frustrated as I was? No relief in sight. And when he finally let go would that make it so much better? Make it explosive?

"That's it, take it all. Feel good?" Yes, I was finally starting to get there. The man's moans and grunts filled my ears, closing me into the fantasy. God, I wanted to hear Matt moan, knowing it was because of me. That I'd made him frustrated and he just couldn't hold it in, the sound escaping him. Until he realized how much I liked it. Then Matt would lean into me, his breath tickling my ear, and let me hear every effect I had on him.

"Matt, please," I groaned into my pillow, shifting to get a better angel, tease my nipples, something that would give me that final push. I was starting to get frustrated by myself with how long I was taking, that I couldn't find the right combo of things to give myself the pleasure I needed. And that frustration would smother everything soon, I couldn't just …

"What was that?"

I think my soul jumped out of my body when I heard Matt's muffled voice from the other side of the door. Not only did my soul jump, but so did my whole body. I jumped, squealed, and shuffled around so that I could sit up, sort of.

"Nothing," I squeaked out, feeling my body heat rise. The buzzing of the vibrator suddenly felt very loud. And the idea of being caught by Matt was exhilarating enough to make my body hum. And the suction cup was suddenly too much. I flexed my hand, needing to get free and turn the vibrator off. But there wasn't anything in my hand. The key was gone.

Fuck.

I shifted left, right, hoping the key would be just on the pillow. But of course, it wasn't there. It probably fell under the bed knowing my luck. And the audio porn kept playing, the smack of skin sharp and alluring. And the toy kept vibrating. And the panic was starting to settle in, making my heart rate go even crazier.

There were two options. Call out for Matt or spend a good amount of time struggling to find the key and contort my body to get it. The first option was … mortifying. But the second option would probably attract his attention anyways.

"Matt?"

"Yeah?"

I winced at the sound of his voice. He was close. Probably right outside the door. Probably could hear the buzzing.

"I'm gonna need your help, but ... you've got to let me explain first."

CHAPTER 4

Matt

I couldn't bring myself to stay at the bar for more than one drink. And that one drink was spent working out the details of taking over Caleb's lease. I had three days to confirm I wanted it and then I'd move in next week.

I knew I should take the place. Knew I'd been mooching off Kasey for too long already. Knew that she'd likely start resenting me if I stayed much longer. But damn it, I didn't really want to move. Would it be that bad if I asked her to just let me stay? If I promised to be better about my shoes, tease her a little less, would she say yes?

Kicking my shoes off in the entryway, I tried to come up with a list of reasons why Kasey should let me stay. I enjoy cooking for her and she seemed to enjoy my cooking. I wasn't afraid of challenging her stubborn loyalty to peanut butter brands. Our chore preferences were compatible, she hated dishes and didn't mind vacuuming, I was the opposite. And even though she would never admit to being afraid of spiders, I would get rid of them for her without giving her a hard time. ... well, the teasing would be limited. I wouldn't be able to resist watching her face shift as she tried to reason why she suddenly left a room. And when she's watching anime or whatever, I could be ...

"Matt, please."

I froze in the middle of the hallway, half convinced I was delusional, half convinced my fantasy of Kasey allowing me to stay as her roommate fast forwarded to other things I wanted from her. Because her voice, while muffled through the door, sounded breathy. Breathy and needy. And if she was needy, I sure as hell wanted to fulfill that need.

"What was that?" My heart thundered as I tried to think of rational explanations for what I heard and not let my brain get carried away with a fantasy. I probably just misheard her. She must've said ... nothing that rhymed with Matt made sense though. And then the horrible idea that maybe she was talking to someone else settled in. Some other Matt, someone with my name but with the envious opportunity to have her body.

"Nothing." Kasey squeaked the word, the sound accompanied by frantic shuffling. Frantic, but not enough noise to support my theory that she had another man over. The amount of relief that brought me was stupidly high and I knew I should go cool my head, take a shower, and forget about the little waver in her voice when she said my name. But my feet were glued in place. I was desperate for just a little more, something to hold on to when I moved to Caleb's. Some sort of chance.

"Matt?"

"Yeah?" Eager, I sounded way too eager.

"I'm gonna need your help, but ... you've got to let me explain first."

Explain? The word echoed in my head, spinning like I would understand what it meant if I just looked at it differently.

"Matt?"

"Sorry, yeah, go ahead." I shook my head, trying to literally shake away the dirty thoughts. But when she started talking again, there was no amount of shaking that could chase away those thoughts.

"I was ... having trouble ... masturbating."

Aw fuck.

"And when I have trouble like this, I tend to need ... extra stimulation."

The slow way she formed the words was torture. Like nails dragging down my chest, painfully erotic.

"So, I ..." Her words trailed off, soft, hesitant, and anxious. I didn't want her to be anxious, not because of me.

"Hey, Kas, I'm not judging you. I know ... I know sharing your home means you don't get the opportunity to ... take care of things like you used to. And that makes the time you do get to ... care for things a little more intimidating, pressuring. I understand." God, did I understand. Obviously, I hadn't brought anyone else back here and by the time I had the energy to go out after moving, I'd gotten to enjoy the quiet nights with Kasey. But she had this one pair of sleep shorts that damn near broke me. They rode up as she shifted around on the couch and when she stood, I could see a cluster of freckles on her ass. I wanted to know how far they went. Wanted to kiss every one of them. I had to wait until she was asleep, then an extra hour, to feel safe enough to hop in the shower and rub one out. I'd even used her damn soap. I felt so guilty, I made her pancakes the next morning with the poor excuse that I was just craving them.

"Okay." Her breathing was heavy enough to come through the door and as I strained to hear every word from her lips, some other sound caught my attention. A buzzing. A low and steady buzzing. Shit. That sound shot straight to my cock. Why hadn't she turned it off when we started talking?

"You see, sometimes it's hard –"

Yeah, it's real fucking hard, Kas.

"– to get there on my own. I get a … knee-jerk reaction and pull away. So, I …"

I was considering how mad she'd be if I just went ahead and opened the door. I mean, it sounded like she wanted me to come in. And this slow explanation was affecting my blood flow. Any more of this and I wouldn't be able to use the head on my shoulders.

"I … handcuffed myself to the headboard."

My head tilted forward, a moment that could only be described as going brain dead for the seconds it took to conjure the image of Kasey tied to her bed. I landed on her door, the thud making Kasey jump on the other side.

"Sorry. I just … so you're stuck like …" Fuck. Was she wearing any clothes? Or maybe just a shirt? I *needed* to fucking see her.

"Um ... yeah. I dropped the key. Behind the bed, I think. I normally keep it looped around my finger but ..." But when I replied to her plea, she jumped and dropped the key.

"So, you want me to come in and find the key?" I should offer to cover my eyes, promise to not look. But I physically couldn't make the words come out. I was desperate to see, to know what she looked like when she was caring for herself. To get any sort of glimpse into what she was like in bed, what she was into.

But if she asked me, if she told me to keep my eyes down, to not look, I would. If she told me, I would.

"Yeah, but first could you ..."

I shouldn't be disappointed. Of course, she'd ask me to avert my eyes one way or another. Kasey didn't want me to see her like that, exposed and intimately vulnerable. That wasn't our relationship. Even though I couldn't think of anything I was more desperate for at the moment.

"Could you take the vibrator out first? It's getting ... really sensitive."

Jesus' fucking Christ.

CHAPTER 5

Kasey

Sensitive wasn't the right word for what I was feeling. Though logically I knew the clit sucker's settings hadn't changed, it sure as hell felt like it had. And talking to Matt was making it worse. The way his voice kept wavering. Did he know what he was doing to me? God, maybe I shouldn't have asked for his help. I could probably squirm my way out of this situation if I tried hard enough. It'd take a lot of time, but surely, it'd be better than this embarrassment.

"Matt, please." I didn't mean to say those words again. But it felt … so much. My nerves jumped from every little pulse, my thighs rubbing together.

"Yeah," he breathed. But when he didn't immediately open the door, I whined. Like a stupid needy child. "Does that mean I can come in now?"

I nodded, then realized how stupid that was and said, "Yes. Please."

When Matt stepped into the room, he didn't so much enter as he did hover in the doorway. His hand stayed on the doorknob, knuckles going white as his eyes raked over my body. I squirmed under his gaze, the non-touch feeling almost as intense as the damn vibrator. I couldn't stay still when he was looking at me like that, eyes dark, chest heaving in an unsteady rhythm, and those arms jerking as he tensed.

"Matt." My voice came out breathy and I hated it. It was his fault, technically. He was the reason I was feeling so frustrated. The reason I couldn't bring someone home. The reason I had to wait for him to be out of the house or hours into sleep was for me to feel comfortable taking care of myself. And the reason why I kept getting distracted from my fantasy, which drove me to this admittedly stupid predicament.

Matt took slow steps towards me, his eyes bouncing from the cuffs to the hard points under my shirt to the vibrator and back again. When I shifted again, his eyes stalled at the vibrator, nostrils flaring. And then when I did my best to stifle a moan, he met my eyes. And then the bastard had the audacity to lick his lips.

Fuck. I hadn't been able to cum, but with him watching I was finally getting close.

"Did you finish?"

"What?" I couldn't possibly have heard that right. He wouldn't ask that while watching me squirming like this, half-naked. And it wasn't any of his business. He shouldn't want to know.

"Your show. The spy thing."

Oh. I get it. He's trying to break the tension. Make things less sexual. Because he probably had zero interest in seeing his roommate/landlord like this.

"No, I hadn't … started it."

Matt paused at the side of my bed, eyes now glued to the toy between my thighs. His brow furrowed.

"Have you been at this since I left?" His eyes met mine and I looked away.

"Not the whole time." And even though I didn't say it, I knew he heard the but. The 'but most of the time.'

"Have you finished, Kasey?"

I couldn't keep my thighs still or bring myself to look at him. But then he gave me no choice. Matt sat on the edge of the bed, one firm hand landing on the vibrator, adding extra pressure. The other hand took my chin and pulled me to look at him.

"Did you come?"

His hand on the toy shifted, pressing the sucker even closer to my clit. I tried not to react. To stifle the noises and keep from jerking away. Because I knew Matt wasn't doing it on purpose. He was entirely focused on me, waiting for my answer. But what would happen when I gave it to him?

"No."

"Do you want to?" Matt leaned in closer, close enough that I could feel his body heat. And smell the beer on his breath.

"You've been drinking."

"I only had one drink."

"But … I … I'm sort of your landlord. That means there's some sort of power imbalance going on." Why was I trying to stop this? I was literally just picturing this man going down on me. If he was offering to deliver my elusive orgasm, I should say yes.

But then what would happen tomorrow? Would I hide in my room until he moved out? Or would he do that?

"You know Caleb?"

"What?" My brow furrowed and I shifted to sit up better, to pull away from his weight on the toy.

"Caleb, one of Dylan's friends." He waited until I nodded to continue, "He's moving and asked if I could take over his lease. No more power imbalance."

"Oh."

This sure as hell wasn't how I pictured him telling me he was moving out. I pictured him making some extravagant meal for dinner, telling me before dessert, and giving me enough time to come up with a way to … say something.

My head started to droop, the rest of my body getting to the numb part of overstimulation. Huh, that was definitely a coincidence and not a reaction.

"Got any other stubborn reasons for me or can I get to work now?" Matt pulled my chin up again. And seeing his bright smile reminded me that that would be gone soon. That he would be gone soon. And that there really wasn't any good reason to say no to something.

"Okay."

"Okay?" Matt's hand moved from my chin, up into my hair, pushing it back then tangling his fingers in. His head tilted and eyes narrowed before he said, "Are you listening to something?"

Oh. I'd completely tuned out the audio porn. But now that he brought it up, I could hear the moans and not-so-innocent squishes. I couldn't tell if it was still the first one on the playlist, but between the sounds were whispered words about how the moment was better than imagined.

"It's …"

Matt took one earbud out and put it in. As the couple started reaching their orgasms, Matt let out a breathy laugh. "Damn, Kasey. I'm not sure what I expected but this … fuck. This wasn't enough to get you off, huh?"

"I'm just –"

"Doesn't matter. I'm doing the work now. Just a few things we gotta take care of first."

"Okay." The numbness was gone, replaced with excitement, my blood rushing in one particular place.

"Are the handcuffs staying on?"

I jerked on the metal gently, testing to see if there was any sting to my skin. There wasn't.

"Yes."

"You said you get the urge to pull away when you're close."

"Yes."

"So will you beg me to stop?"

I sucked my breath in. Matt was so close that I could taste his breath. He'd had something hoppy at the bar. I bet I could taste it if I kissed him.

"Kasey?"

"Yes."

"Yes, what?"

"Yes, I'll probably ask you to stop."

Matt's jaw twitched, the fingers in my hair

tightening. "And will you actually want me to stop?"

"No."

Matt's head fell to my shoulder, a mumbled curse slipping from his lips, tickling my skin. "Okay. Stoplight system, yeah? Green means go, red means stop?"

"Okay."

"Kasey." Matt sat back up, a stern look in his eyes.

"Green."

"Good, and if your mouth is otherwise occupied, three taps."

Just the thought of Matt putting anything in my mouth had me salivating. And I nodded a little too eagerly. But that made him smile and any cringe behavior was worth that smile.

"That's my girl." With that very butterfly-inducing phrase, Matt turned up the vibrator and started grinding it. "Now, how far do you want this to go? Are we having sex? Or am I just getting you off real good?"

"Sex. I want sex. With you."

Matt was moving slowly, rocking in time with the new audio that had begun. Something about just testing things out with a kiss. I couldn't pay attention to it with Matt in front of me. With Matt looking at me like he was going to eat me up.

"Condom?"

I tilted my head to the bedside table and Matt let go of my hair to open the drawer. I watched his eyes trail over the other items in the drawer before he shook his head and pulled out a condom. He set the foil on the table and his hand returned to me. But instead of returning to my hair, his hand slipped under my shirt, grazing up and down my side. It was the lightest of touch, so little pressure that it felt like a breeze tickling my skin. But it made me burn. Made my hips start lifting to meet his hand.

"Hard no's?"

His fingertips started to focus on my breast, light strokes that curved along my skin. My eyes drifted close as he continued. The audio had shifted to the girl getting on her knees, the man saying something about how she didn't have to, didn't expect her to, or something. I was just picturing Matt standing up, pushing down his pants, and pulling my chin to face him and his ...

But then Matt's hands were off me and the visual broke. My eyes burst open to see Matt had leaned away from me, his arms crossed and fingers fisted into his sleeves. He leaned back in, still not touching me, and said, "Hard no's, Kasey. Can't go any further until you tell me."

"Um ..." I shifted underneath him and Matt's hand went back to the toy. My hips rose eagerly, but when he turned the vibrator completely off instead of moving it, I plopped back to the bed with a huff.

"If you're not comfortable telling me, then we're not doing this."

I huffed again, but took a deep breath and started through my list. "Smacking and biting is fine, but nothing that'll leave a mark after a few hours. No anal sex today. No degradation. And ..."

I bit my lip. It wasn't a no, so much as a boundary

I needed to keep in place so the inevitable move out and subsequent lack of contact didn't hurt so much.

"And?" Matt prompted. He leaned even closer, his breath tickling my lips. And I knew he was going to do it and it was now or never.

"And no kissing."

CHAPTER 6

Matt

I pulled away from Kasey to get a good look at her face. But she was biting her lip, making direct eye contact. She was serious. No kissing. And she said it along with her hard no's.

"No kissing? At all?" I'm not sure I'd be able to do that. Not when my cock was buried inside her. My mouth would need to be on her skin one way or another.

"Just not on my …" She looked down at where my hand laid on the vibrator and I moved it away. "Just not on my face."

Face. Okay. I could certainly handle that, but … fuck I wanted to kiss her into a damn stupor. If that was her condition, maybe I should stop here. Walk out without a word and make her come to me. Make her want to kiss me.

"What about you?"

"What?" Was she asking how I felt about the kissing thing? Was this the kind of thing where she didn't want it unless I wanted it enough to argue for it?

"What are you hard no's?"

Of course. Kasey was too straightforward for those kinds of mental gymnastics.

"I don't think that's necessary. It'd be a little difficult for you to cross my boundaries like that." I nodded to the handcuffs and she looked up at them, shaking her arms slightly and making the chain clink against the frame. With her looking up, her neck was exposed and since she'd already cleared up her nos, I couldn't stop myself. I leaned in, pressing light kisses down her throat, then licked back up. And I was rewarded with the sweetest gasp and her body shivering underneath me. I repeated the pattern on the other side of her neck and turned the toy back on. Her hips jerked as I started rocking the vibrator inside her, hopefully rubbing against her g-spot, it was hard to tell seeing as I only knew what the 'exterior' part of the toy looked like.

"Matt," Kasey whined. My breath was already coming in heavy waves but her sounds had me fucking panting. And the porn she was listening to had shifted to the woman getting head. Which sounded like an excellent fucking idea.

"Still want to waste time listing my no's?" I sat up and wedged a knee between her thighs, pushing forward so the toy rested against my leg and she could grind to her heart's content. Then I lifted her shirt, rolling it up and pressing it into her hands to hold.

I knew there wasn't anything under the shirt, but that hadn't prepared me for the mouth-watering sight of her bare breasts shifting with her breathing. Resisting temptation, I rested my hands on her waist and pulled her up to grind the vibrator against me. I wasn't confident this angle would work, but those fears were quickly assuaged as Kasey started moving, setting her own, quicker pace. As I leaned down to kiss her neck again, I considered forcing her to slow down. I fully intended to make her come as many damn times as I could, but that didn't mean I couldn't draw it out. Make this moment last as long as it could.

"Matt, tell me." Kasey's voice came out breathless, her eyes half closed and rolled back.

I wished she was asking me to tell her how bad I wanted her, how bad I need to have my hands and mouth all over her body. And how badly I didn't want to leave, had only been partially considering it, and only said it so that I'd at least have that opportunity.

But I knew Kasey. And I knew that wasn't what she meant.

"Well, I'm okay with markings, though I don't see how you could manage that. I have no interest in impact play, in either direction. And I'm also not interested in getting it in the ass." I laughed as Kasey began to shake her head. "Oh yeah? That a deal breaker for you, Kas. Not sure how you were planning on pegging me like this."

"No, I said I couldn't do anal today. I'm into it as long as ..."

"As long as what?"

"As long as I've had time to prep and my pussy still gets attention." Fucking Christ. I'd long since gotten hard, but the ache in my pants was growing needier with every word.

"Good to know," I murmured, kissing down her

neck to her collarbone, tracing the lines of it with my tongue.

"But not today." She said the words quickly and I pulled back so she could see me nod and repeat the words back to her. "Not today."

She stared at me for a second longer before nodding and letting her head fall back. I returned my mouth to her chest, moving from her collarbone to between her breasts. And since she had her own rhythm down, I let my hands trail up from her waist to her tits, reveling in the softness. I kneaded her breast, kissing up to one nipple while my other hand thumbed the other. Gentle strokes on each side made Kasey whimper and her hands jerk again. I let myself imagine she wanted to touch me, wanted to run her fingers through my hair and grip, maybe scratch up my back.

"You going to come for me?" Most of the words from the headphones were tuned out, but something about the line stuck out. Maybe it was because Kasey's hips stilled. I turned off the vibrator and shifted back, braced over her so that I wasn't pressed against her anymore.

"What's not working?"

Kasey sucked in her breath and looked away. Then, in a voice too small for the woman I knew, "It's just taking so long."

"There's no rush, Kas. I mean, I just got here. So at least for me, we just got started."

"I've listened to at least two clips of couples reaching climax before me." The words came out gritted and tears were starting to form in the corner of her eyes.

If she hadn't said no, I would've kissed them away.

"Well, they're actors, right? It's a performance."

"It's all your fault. You and your stupid arms and your stupid pajama pants. And now you're just here but it's not right."

I wanted to ask what made my arms and pajama pants so stupid, but there was something more important in that tangent. "What's not right?"

Kasey looked back at me, eyes looking up and down my body. "You're clothes. I'm naked and handcuffed. And you're fully clothed, in fucking jeans. Jeans are like the furthest thing from being undressed."

"I could be in a tux." I knew I shouldn't, but I couldn't help the smile that pulled my lips. I stood up and started to strip for her.

"Tuxes are at least softer," she murmured, but her eyes followed my hands, watching as I pulled my shirt away. I didn't particularly think about the way women saw my body. Either they liked it or they didn't and that was all there was to it. But I ate up the way Kasey was looking at me, eyes lusted over, chest rising, licking her lips, thighs rubbing together. And when I stood back up from pulling down my pants and underwear, Kasey let out a whispered, "Fuck."

My dick bobbed, an eager little fucker desperate for Kasey's attention. Any time I pictured this moment, it was frantic. There wasn't any time for a perusal of our bodies, there was just need. But this … this was a moment frozen in time to absorb every inch of each other.

I stepped back up to the bed and took her phone

from the table. "This where the audio's coming from?" When she nodded, I unlocked her phone and scrolled through the playlist options. Looking for something that was long and had less of a chance of making her feel pressured. I could feel Kasey's eyes on my cock, watching as it twitched in reaction to some of the descriptions.

"Can I ..." Kasey shifted closer to the edge, scooting so that she was almost laying down, her eyes level with my dick. "Just while you're picking something else."

Fuck, how could I say no to that?

CHAPTER 7

Kasey

Matt's dick was hypnotizing. And mouth-watering. And slightly curved upwards. And veiny. And really fucking hard. And while he was scrolling through the porn, it twitched excitedly. I mean, how could I not want it in my mouth? And after all, he seemed dedicated to getting me there, so I should reward him accordingly.

"Can I ..." I scooted to the side of the bed and slid as far down as I could without straining my arms. The position put me on level with his cock, which seemed to jump at my unspoken request. "Just while you're picking something else."

Matt stepped up to the bed, free hand stroking my face. It was sweet, but with the salty musk of his cock just *right there*, it wasn't what I wanted. I leaned forward and stuck my tongue out to lick him from base to head. Matt's eyes rolled back and he teetered forward slightly, his hand moving from my cheek to tighten in my hair. And while he was close enough now that I could get him in my mouth, I repeated the action instead, adding slow zigzags. Matt stopped scrolling through the playlists and I hummed in approval.

"You taste amazing, Matt."

His cock twitched again and this time I sucked his head into my mouth. Matt's fingers tightened in my hair, stinging deliciously, telling me that he liked what I was doing. I rubbed circles over his head with the flat of my tongue before leaning further to slide him all the way into my mouth.

"Christ," Matt muttered. He looked down at me, eyes even darker, and shifted closer, pushing his cock further into my mouth. I wasn't taking all of him yet, but I already needed to be conscious about my breathing. Slow breaths through my nose, relaxing my throat, just so I could take a little bit more. I wanted just a little bit more.

"If you weren't literally being held back, you'd have already made me blow, wouldn't you?"

I hummed in reply and tilted my head to start sucking, but Matt held me off. He pressed something on my phone and set it down. The soft smacking of lips started playing. And while the kissing sounds from the other file set me off since I couldn't kiss Matt, these sounds just made me more eager to suck his cock. I guess as long as I had my mouth on him, the fact that I shouldn't kiss him didn't matter.

"Can you still tap like this?" Matt asked, the words groaned out as I started swirling my tongue along the bottom of his shaft. When I didn't immediately respond, Matt pulled away until his cock was out of my mouth, lines of saliva dripping between us, connecting us. "Christ, Kas, that's hot as fuck, but I need to make sure you're good."

"I'm good, but I was better with your cock in my mouth."

"Kas," he warned. I sighed but tilted my hand back so I could knock on the wall. Twice. "Good girl."

My pussy throbbed in response. And the feeling doubled as Matt leaned over and put one hand on the vibrator. My hips lifted, eager to feel the vibrations again. But Matt didn't turn it on. He took it out. He watched as the toy pulled free, licking his lips. Matt brought it up to his face, examining the lines of wetness that dripped to his fingers. God, how had I gotten so wet but hadn't come? It was so damn …

"My turn to taste you," Matt said, right before he put the vibrator in his mouth and all those stupid thoughts shut up real quick. His tongue peeked out, wrapping around the toy, licking it clean. When he pulled it out, there was a light sheen of saliva. Matt licked his lips and leaned down, pressing his forehead against mine. For a second, I thought he was going to kiss me. His lips were right there and I wanted them. Wanted to taste myself on him, pretend like that meant he was mine.

"Matt," I breathed. My lips moved, but I couldn't form the words. I wanted his lips on mine so badly but my brain was hung up on a kiss' ability to change things.

"Don't worry, Kas. I didn't forget." Matt gave me a crooked, half smile. Then he dipped his head down and restarted that neck thing he was doing before. The way his tongue glided across my skin made goosebumps bloom. As I started shivering from his touch, one of his hands trailed down my side, the touch feather-light. He went up and down, slow strokes that had me panting in a matter of seconds.

"You're so reactive for me, pet." The voice on the audio was rough, kind of like how Matt sounded after a run.

"What did you put on?"

"Hmm. I'm not sure, I was a little distracted." His hand stopped its lazy stroking and gripped my hip. His lips moved further down, sucking one nipple into his mouth sharply. I gasped, arching my back for more. "But it seems to be working, huh?"

Matt's hand slipped from my hip to my thighs. He pushed my leg aside and did the soft stroking thing, teasing the sensitive skin there.

"Matt, please."

He didn't respond. Instead, he sucked harder, eliciting a sharp cry. My body swung between squirming away and arching into his warm touch. He sucked until I was whimpering, then sucked and pulled, my nipple falling out of my mouth with a pop.

"Sorry, what was that? Why don't you tell me while I work the other side?"

His warm tongue wrapped around the other nipple and I cried his name again. Meanwhile, his hand on my thigh had started to focus on the bit of skin where my thigh met my groin. His hand rested there, thumb stroking up and down, up and down. So damn close.

"Stay open for me princess, let me play with you." What the fuck was this playlist Matt had picked out? And how the fuck had he picked something that was exactly what I needed in the moments I lost focus?

Finally, when tears started to form at the corners of my eyes, Matt let go and stilled his hand. "What were you trying to say before?"

His smile was brighter as he looked up, a mischievous glint in his eyes.

"I thought I was going to suck your dick some more."

"Yeah, but that was before I got a taste of you. You're so fucking delicious, I needed to get my mouth on you. And I wanted you to be dripping when I do." Matt's hand moved to my pussy, one finger circling my entrance. He dipped the finger in and quickly pulled it out. Matt held his finger between us. It glistened in the dim light of my bedside lamp.

"Taste yourself, Kasey. Taste just how God damn good you are." Matt held his finger to my lips and I opened my mouth immediately. I licked up his long finger once before he tilted it so I could suck him in. My mouth watered as I caressed his finger with my tongue. And I'd probably crave the combination of our salty flavors for a long, long time.

"Suck harder, Kas. Give me a glimpse of what I'm missing."

I took a shaky breath before complying, my cheeks hollowing as I sucked. I twisted my tongue around his finger, moaning when his eyes drooped. I pulled my head back, making a pop as his finger slid out.

"Now be a good boy and eat me out."

CHAPTER 8

Matt

I almost didn't hear what Kasey said after she sucked my finger. I was having a hard time breathing, let alone listening. But thank God I heard it.

"Now be a good boy and eat me out."

"Yes, ma'am." I grinned, remembering how barely five hours ago she was glaring at me for calling her that. Now her eyes were completely lusted over, her lips slick, and her hips lifting. If only I could die the second I have to leave this room, then I could be truly happy.

I grabbed one of her extra pillows and repositioned myself on the bed. I could already see her glistening cunt and I was fucking eager for it. I practically shoved the pillow under her hips and threw her legs over my shoulder. I wanted these thighs to squeeze me within an inch of my life. I wanted to hear her whimper, see her tear up like she did when I was sucking her tits. She was gonna come on my mouth or I was gonna smother myself to death here.

Kasey watched me as I settled between her thighs and examined my meal. Her breath was already ragged, heavy waves through her body. I leaned forward, reveling in the way Kasey shook at my approach. But an inch away, I turned my head, kissing up her thigh to her knee. And then I turned the other way and kissed down from her knee. I looked up to Kasey to see her hands quivering above her head, lip sucked between her teeth.

"You're beautiful like this," I said at the same time she whispered, "You're so pretty between my thighs."

Fuck this woman had me.

I didn't have it in me to draw this out, to tease her anymore. I slid my hands under her ass, gripping tight, then loosening once my brain caught up and reminded me that she said no marks. With reckless abandon, I took one long lick up her pussy and groaned. She tasted so damn perfect. And the way she screamed my name and squirmed had me practically humping the bed. I'd only gotten one fucking taste and she was already like this. What was she going to be like when she finally came?

"You want my mouth off this pussy, you know what to say." I spoke into her, not able to pull myself away.

"Matt, please."

"Please what?" I hovered over her, preparing myself to pull away when she asked.

"Stop teasing me."

Fuck yes.

I didn't have any sort of finesse, I just opened my mouth and sucked and licked and lost my goddamn mind. When she started to shake, I pinned one arm across her stomach, partly because she told me she needs that restraint, but mostly because if I didn't get my fill of this pussy, I was gonna turn into some sort of savage caveman that couldn't think of anything except fucking his woman. And Kasey wasn't my woman. Currently. But maybe if I made this good for her, she'd consider it after I moved out.

"God, you make me feel so good," a woman on the audio said. I got why Kasey listened to this now. I didn't really hear it until my mind drifted and then it reeled me right back in place. Like bumpers for bowling, it kept my head out of the gutter. Well, a different kind of gutter.

Letting go of her ass, I brought two fingers to her entrance, circling, dipping in just a bit and pushing against the edges. While my fingers made their slow perusal, I settled my mouth on her clit. My tongue swirled around the bundle of nerves and her pussy fluttered against my fingers.

And then, because I knew it would make her scream, I plunged my fingers into her and sucked her clit.

"Matt, fuck that's good!" she screamed.

I groaned into her, overwhelmed by her taste, her reactions, and the ache in my balls that said I needed to be inside her now. God, it's gonna feel so fucking good. But no way in hell was I gonna risk coming first like that. As it was, I wasn't confident I'd be more than a one-pump chump.

So, with the goal of not embarrassing myself in mind, I refocused on fingering her, on finding that spongy spot. I pushed my fingers up inside her sliding up with a light pressure until I found the rougher patch. No wonder she was having so much trouble before, that vibrator was hitting too high. No worries though, I could hit it just right for her.

I shifted my weight to keep her pinned down, then pulsed my fingers against that spot. Kasey jerked, but I held her firm, even though those little whimpers made me want to crawl up her, pound into her, and hold her close, tell her I'll take care of everything. I kept up the pulsing, a quick rhythm that matched her heavy breathing, and sucked at her clit lazily. Too much too soon might overwhelm her, make her feel like I was rushing her. And that was the exact opposite of what I intended.

I watched Kasey's chest rise and fall, a little bereft that I couldn't see her face. But watching her breath slowly quicken was all I needed. I switched from pulsing to rubbing small circles and copying the motion on her clit with the flat of my tongue.

"Fuck. That. Keep doing that."

"Yes, ma'am." I didn't make a single change, not even speeding up when she started clenching my fingers. It was so tempting when she was this close, to push for that finish line. But that didn't work for Kasey before. I could hold back for now. Lord knows I wouldn't be able to when I was balls deep in her.

Hmm. How did I want to fuck her? There were only so many positions we could do with her cuffed like this. And I didn't want to take her from behind. I wanted to see her face at least once while she came for me. I loved watching her face. I'll miss it when I move.

"Matt, it's too much. I can't," Kasey whined. Her thighs started squirming around my head, then squeezed, then squirmed some more. Her body was shaking, right on the line of bliss.

"Yes, you can, Kas. Show me." I circled her g-spot faster and switched between swirling her clit with my tongue to sucking it sharply. And for good measure, I abandoned the hold on her waist and reached for her breast, kneading the soft flesh for a moment before pinching her nipple.

"Matt!" she cried as her pussy convulsed around my fingers and her body shook. I pulled my fingers out and quickly replaced them with my tongue. So fucking wet and delicious. More. I need more of this. Was it too much to ask to keep eating her?

"Matt, I – fuck, I actually came." Her voice was light, a little puff of laughter. And when I managed to pull myself away from her pussy, I could see a soft smile lighting her face. She didn't smile much and I followed the curves of her lips closely, hoping to memorize it.

"Yeah, I was watching. Tasted real good too. Now, can you get up on your knees and face the headboard?"

Kasey's head tilted, brows furrowing for a moment before she turned and got up to her knees. I got behind her, running my hands up from her thighs to her breast. She was so fucking hot against my palms. Hot, soft flesh. And it turned out those freckles on the bottom of her ass were just a small cluster, a dusting of temptation, a mark I wanted to bite.

"Matt?"

"Yes, ma'am?" One hand trailed back down,

pushing her legs apart before palming her cunt. My other hand spread across her collarbone, softly stroking her thundering pulse with my thumb.

"Are you ... going to put the condom on?"

I dipped the tips of three fingers in and Kasey shook so hard I had to lean her against me to keep her up.

"I will. When I'm ready to fuck you." I grinded my cock against her ass, her soft flesh a sanctuary for my hardness. Christ. I slid my fingers further inside her, stroking that sweet spot.

"You feel ready to me," Kasey murmured, rocking her ass against me.

"Maybe. But don't you think it'd be better if you came one more time?"

"I want your cock though."

"Then you know what to do to get it." I pressed my palm against her clit, shifting till I could feel the swollen nerves pulse against my skin. Then I stroked her g-spot faster and pressed my mouth to her neck. It didn't take long this time for her to shake violently and soak my fingers again.

"Thatta girl," I whispered in her ear, holding my wet fingers in front of her face. She opened her mouth and like a magnet, my fingers went to her lips, letting her suck her come from them, even when my mouth watered for the taste. My dick twitched against her ass, beyond ready to be inside her, to feel her come around it.

"I came for you, so be a good boy and fuck me now."

CHAPTER 9

Kasey

"Yes, ma'am."

I couldn't see him, but I could hear his smile. His hands went to my waist and he shifted and turned so that he was seated under me, my legs over his waist. Like this, his face was so close. I could kiss him. All I'd have to do was lean forward, just a little bit.

Matt gave me another cocky smile and reached to the bedside. Condom in hand, he held the corner of it up to my mouth. "I just wanna see you open it."

I wanted to roll my eyes, say something snarky, but fuck, I understood it. I bit the corner of the wrapper and pulled. The foil ripped and I let go.

"Put it on."

Matt threw the wrapper to the side and put the condom on. I watched as the latex spread over his cock and my pussy clenched around nothing. Close, I was so close to having Matt inside me.

"Kasey." Matt let go of his cock and put his hands on my waist. "You still want this? I won't be mad or anything if you're satisfied now and don't want to go any farther."

"Matt, I won't be satisfied until I come on your cock."

That smile. I was going to miss that smile when he was gone.

Matt's hands moved to my hips and gripped tightly. Then with a whispered, "Yes, ma'am," he dragged me down onto his dick. And I screamed, a wave of pleasure crashing over me as my clit grinded into his pelvis and he filled me.

"Did you just come again?"

I rested my head against his shoulder and tried to catch my breath. "Don't get a big head. You don't have some magic dick or something. Your pelvis just rubbed against my clit the right way."

"You mean that clit I made all nice and swollen with my mouth." Matt pulled my hips up and slammed down again. "And here I was worried about being a one-pump chump."

"Shut up, Matt." Again, he pulled me up and down, setting up a merciless rhythm.

"You sure about that? I think you like it when I talk, when I make noise for you. That's the appeal of the audio, isn't it?"

"Yes." The word was barely more than a breath as Matt started rocking into me.

"Good. Cause I have to tell you how fucking amazing you feel. I knew you were gonna squeeze me nice and tight, but shit, Kas. You feel like heaven."

"Matt ..." Words were so hard. I wanted to tell him

how good he felt, how good he had been making me feel. But if I did that, it might turn into begging him to stay. And that was stupid. And a stupid thing to say with his cock inside me. So instead, I said, "Let go, Matt. Let me ride you."

Matt's hands fell away, balling up in the sheets. "Yes, ma'am."

He was having too much fun with that. But the way he said it, like he was willing to do anything I asked, made it more soothing than before. And I wanted to make his compliance worth it.

I shifted my knees and braced my biceps on Matt's shoulders. He watched my every move with heavy-lidded eyes, his chest rising in quick waves. As I started rocking my hips, Matt let out a low groan. His head fell back, his Adam's apple bobbing. And I couldn't help it. I needed my mouth on him. Sucking his cock for barely a minute wasn't nearly enough. I needed to taste him, bite him. Leave a little mark that would fade too quickly for my liking.

"Shit, Kas," Matt moaned when I licked his throat. And then that sound turned into something closer to a growl when I bit him. Not hard, just enough to feel his skin squish.

Matt's hips started quivering, sharp jerks like he was trying to keep from moving, but he just couldn't. I sucked at his neck, bouncing faster. I could feel his dick twitch inside me and I wanted it.

I moved to his ear, sucking it into my mouth and letting out a deep moan when he started thrusting again. "Matt, come for me."

"Kas, not yet. I don't want to come yet. I want to be inside you a little longer." Matt's hands returned to my skin, one tangling into my hair, his arm pressing me closer to him. And his other hand went between us, resting on my clit and rubbing fast circles. "How bout you come for me first?"

I didn't have much choice in the matter. At this point my clit was so sensitive, one touch had me halfway there already. My only hope was that my quickly oncoming orgasm would spur his own. I wanted to see it, see that smile fade to unabashed pleasure. Hear his groans. I'd be masturbating to that moment for a long time.

The flutters started fast and Matt's grip on my hair tightened. Kiss. I wanted to kiss him as I came.

"Matt." He looked at me, eyes wild. I didn't say anything else, just pressed my lips to his. I think I came when our mouths parted and our tongues met. Or maybe it was when he sighed into my mouth or tilted my head to deepen the kiss. It didn't really matter when I came, the moment was so all-encompassing because he tasted like mine.

"Did you just come?" I asked when we were too out of breath to keep kissing. I could feel the heat of his come dripping down through the condom.

"Yeah. And you *can* get a big head about it. Because you do have a magical pussy. And lips. Can I kiss you some more?"

"But we're done. You came." I didn't understand. Why did he want more when this was just about getting each other off? He was moving, so why was he prolonging this?

Matt laughed, soft and sad, then ducked under my arms to pull away. "You can just say no, Kas."

I didn't say no. But he was already off the bed before I could form words to explain my confusion. He bent down and came back up with the key to my cuffs in hand. Matt smoothed my hair, tucking stray ends behind my ears before undoing the lock. I sat back on my feet, my now free hands falling to my lap. Matt turned away from me, bending over to gather his clothes. I watched, unmoving, as he got dressed and walked out of my room without looking back.

And fuck, all that frustration I'd been feeling since Matt took up residence in my guest room, came right back. And it was somehow so much worse now.

CHAPTER 10

Matt

When she kissed me, I thought things were starting to look different for Kasey. That she realized she wanted more. That I had somehow fucked her well enough that she wouldn't want to let go. In retrospect, that was a little cocky of me to think. Kasey was stubborn. And fully capable of finding someone to fulfill her sexual needs when she didn't have a roommate cockblocking her.

And now it's been two days and the only contact I had with Kasey was a very thorough moving-out checklist she emailed me and mumbled hellos when she broke her bedroom sequester. At this rate, the next time I'd have a full-blown conversation with her would be when Dylan convinced her to come out to a party. And that only happened, like, once a year.

I knew she was more of an introvert, but I thought she'd gotten used to me being here, started to like having the neutral, comfortable company that normally only came after years of dating. But maybe that was just me. Maybe I made her uncomfortable, unable to relax in her own home.

Resigned to my fate, I pulled out my phone and texted Caleb about coming over to see his apartment later today. I should tell him I'd take it. There's no way I'd find a better place. And obviously, Kasey didn't want me around.

It's just … why the fuck would she have let me fuck her if she was going to feel uncomfortable afterward? She only wanted to go forward if I wasn't her 'tenant'. But if it was just sex for her, if she really didn't care, why was she avoiding me?

"God damn it, Matt!"

Like an eager little pup, I ran when she called my name. Even though she sounded mad. Pissed off and yelling was better than nothing.

When I stepped out of my room, Kasey was standing at the entryway, kicking my shoes. I could've sworn I'd toed them into the little shelves. Pretty sure. But the way Kasey was grumbling, pushing my shoes into the cubby with her feet instead of bending to pick them up, made it hard to care. She was so cute when she got all flustered and grumpy like that.

"Stop that!" Kasey yelled. I leaned against the wall, watching. She crossed her arms and huffed. Then, seemingly uncomfortable, moved her hands to her hips.

"Stop what? Leaving my shoes in the middle of the floor? I'm sorry about that Kas, but you won't have to deal with it much longer. Gonna go talk to Caleb later today." I tried to keep up an easy smile but reminding myself that I'd be gone soon made my whole body twitch.

"I'm not talking about your damn shoes. That, stop doing that." She pointed to me, gesturing vaguely before huffing.

"You're gonna have to be clearer." I put my hands in my pocket to resist the urge to grab her outstretched hand.

"That. Stop twitching your arms. It's frustrating. You're so frustrating." Kasey crossed her arms again and bit her lip. And then her thighs rubbed together. Huh.

"You're cute when you're frustrated with me." I stepped closer to her and she stepped back. Her breathing was getting heavy. And when I took another step and put a hand on her waist, she nearly stopped breathing altogether.

"Don't do that. We're not fucking again. You're leaving."

"I don't see how those two things connect." I pulled her against me, making her gasp. "We could be a couple. I've already seen you on your crabbiest days and in your rattiest PJs. I know how damn stubborn you are about certain food brands and what number the volume or temperature should be set at. And you know how well I can make you come. Seems like it wouldn't be a hard transition."

I might as well be on my knees begging. Because I knew if she said no, that'd be it. I'd blown my chances of staying friends by asking for more.

"I don't do relationships." Kasey avoided looking me in the eyes, biting her lip harder.

"Why not?"

"I'm no … good at relationships."

"Why do you think that?"

"I don't … I forget to call or text. I get hyper-fixated on work or some inane shit and I forget about people. And then whoever I'm with gets rightfully pissed that I didn't remember to talk to them for weeks. And you're … you, you're the type to go all in with a relationship, the good morning texts every day, the hours-long phone calls, the plans every weekend. You're going to get annoyed when I don't text you back for days or when I choose to watch TV over going out with you. And you'll get lonely when I admit I forgot things, like dates or anniversaries or birthdays. Once you move out, it won't work."

I could definitely see those things wrecking Kasey's previous relationships. Hell, if I started dating Kasey before staying in her guestroom, I would've been hurt by the way she acts sometimes, the losing track of time, the not seeing the importance of going out to a friend's party. But I knew her now, at least well enough to understand that those things weren't a reflection of her values. And if it was the memory issues she was focused on …

"All I'm hearing is that as long as I make sure you remember me, this could work."

"That's not … I'm just an out of sight out of mind kind of person. That's not something you can change."

"Then I just have to make sure the memories are within sight, right?" I gripped her thighs and pulled up, guiding her to wrap her legs around my waist. "I don't mind a little hard work, not when it comes to you. Why don't we start here, on this entryway table? Make a memory so good your face will burn every time you pass by."

I pushed aside the mail and keys and set her ass on the table. I looped my fingers into her shorts and pulled. "Lift your ass, Kas."

"Matt, I don't ..." she started but still braced her hands on the table to lift up.

"Same words as last time, yeah?" I pulled down her shorts and panties, tossing them away and sliding my hands up and down her thighs. Goosebumps spread across her skin as her breathing became unsteady.

"You're lucky I'm horny or else I'd kick you out right now," she grumbled.

"If that's what gives me a chance to show you we could date, then I'm very lucky. But let me tell you how this is gonna go. I'm gonna eat you out for a bit, cause I've been wanting another taste of that sweet pussy. And then I'm gonna make you scream on my cock. And then I'm gonna leave for the day. Maybe the whole night. I'll decide later. And while I'm gone, I want you to distract yourself, forget all about me. And when I get back, you're going to admit you missed me." And if she missed me badly enough, maybe she'd ask me to stay.

I sank to my knees and pushed her legs open. Licking my lips, I ran my fingers up and down her thighs, making long ovals. I looked up to Kasey and smiled when I saw her head was tipped back, eyes closed.

"Kasey?"

"What?" She opened her eyes halfway, looking down at me, impatience written all over her face.

"Do you agree?" I let my fingers go up higher, just enough so that my knuckles brushed against her center.

"Agree to what?"

"That if you miss me while I'm gone today, we'll start dating? And to be clear, when I say dating, I mean the I'm yours and you're mine type of dating. I'm not expecting elaborate dates, in fact, the only difference I'm expecting is that I get to please this pussy. The only one who pleases it."

"Yes," Kasey breathed and as soon as she did, I pulled her cunt open. I rubbed her lips, dipping my fingertips into her wetness. I don't know if it was a reflection of how bad she wanted me or if it was just like she said, that she was horny, but either way, the sight of it made my cock stiffen and ache for her. And that ache got a whole lot worse when I leaned in and started tonguing her.

"Matt!" she screamed, fingers digging into my hair, a sharp pull that spurred me on. With one hand, I pushed one of her legs open, and with the other, I gathered her wetness and circled her clit. My fingers moved slowly, but she was already starting to squirm. Her other leg, draped over my shoulder, squeezed against my head.

"Matt, touch yourself while you eat me out."

Oh fuck. I lifted my eyes to her. She was watching me, hands loosening their hold on my hair. She started stroking my hair, the touch soft and gentle and downright loving.

I let go of her leg and jerked down my zipped, pushing my clothes down just enough that I could pull out my cock. As I started stroking, Kasey shivered. She couldn't even see me follow her instructions. But knowing I did, made her hotter, wetter.

"Such a good boy," she whispered.

"Yeah, just for you, Kas. Such a good boy that I'll come back as soon as you call for me. Whenever you call for me. Even if you forget about me, I'll be right back here on my knees to make you remember."

I swapped my hand on her clit for my mouth, swirling my tongue in quick circles before sucking hard. When her fingers started pulling my hair again and she started whimpering, I slowly slid two fingers into her pussy. I went straight for her g-spot, stroking it in time with how I stroked myself, fast and desperate. I couldn't hold back from switching to rubbing circles inside her, knowing it would get me to that delicious taste quicker, especially since her pussy was already fluttering.

One of Kasey's hands fell from my hair and clutched my shirt, pulling. "Matt, now."

"No." I let go of my dick and grabbed her ass, pulling her closer to me, readying to drown in her pussy. "I have a rule for my girlfriends, Kas. And that's that they come before I get it in."

"That's a dumb rule. What if I just wanna get railed?"

"I suppose I can make exceptions every once in a while. But not now. Now you're going to come on my face so that every time you set your keys down, you have something to remember me by."

CHAPTER 11

Kasey

Matt must be the only man who can tell me to come at the right moment. Because as soon as he said I was going to come on his face, I did. I'd wanted to be stubborn, make him break his stupid rule, and give me his cock. But I couldn't hold back. It hit me like a crash, sharp and sudden. All I could do was try not to squirm off the table as the relief washed through me.

Matt didn't move his mouth from my clit as he watched me convulse, his eyes soft and a smile tugging at the corner of his lips. "Well do I get your cock now? Or you going to ramble on again about how memorable fucking you is?"

He sucked on my clit one last time, letting go with one loud pop before standing. Matt pulled a condom from his pocket, opening it with his mouth. He pulled out the condom and spit the wrapper away before asking, "Are you saying you don't remember the other night?"

I swallowed, watching him roll the condom on.

"How I fucked you so good, you forgot you didn't want to kiss me?"

Stupid man. Stupid man I desperately wanted to kiss again. Stupid man focusing on the wrong part of what I'd said.

Matt's hand went under my knees, holding me up and open for him. "I was a good boy for you, now be a good girl for me and guide me in."

Stupid, rude man who said things that made my pussy flutter.

I reached between us and took hold of his dick. As his head rubbed against my clit, I tightened my grip around his thick hardness and stroked. He'd already spent so much time worshiping my pussy, it was a shame I'd barely been able to look at his cock. He was so warm through the condom. And he was twitching a lot.

"Kas, put me in, please." Matt's voice was verging on pleading, a shaky tone I'd never heard from him before. So even though I wanted to touch him more, I moved his head to my entrance and watched him glide into me. He went slow, his hips quivering after each inch he sank. And when he was fully inside me, he wrapped his arms around my shoulders, holding me tightly as he dragged my ass to the edge of the table. My legs wrapped around him, clutching tightly.

"Kas, I'm gonna be a little rough with you, you say the word and I'll stop. I think you're used to people letting you push them away, even though that's not really what you're doing. You just have different ways to fill your social needs." Matt buried his face in my neck, kissing the sensitive skin under my ear.

"Is that what you were thinking about while eating me out?" So much talking about my stupid habits and not enough fucking. My lack of desire for social interaction wasn't even the real problem here. Well, it wouldn't be if he wasn't moving.

"Yeah. But you wanna know what else I was thinking about?"

"Yes." The word turned into a scream as Matt pulled his hips back, then thrust back into me hard. The table shook underneath me, the loose keys and mail falling off.

"I wondered if you'd kiss me again while you were coming on my cock."

Stupid man, with his stupid obsession with me kissing him. It was stupid how much I wanted to too. How the more he talked, the more I realized he did know me well enough to know what to expect. We could be together without me feeling like I had to perform. But if it worked out like that, then he might as well not move at all. I didn't want him to go.

I wrapped my arms around him, clutching his shirt tightly as he continued steadily pounding into me. When he pushed all the way back in, he would twist his pelvis, grinding against my clit.

"Christ, Kas. You're fucking incredible," Matt whispered. His thrusting paused and he switched to just grinding into me, little circles that rubbed my insides in just the right way. "Don't make me come yet, though. I want this to last a little longer."

"I don't want you to hold back, though."

Matt pulled his head away from my neck and

looked at me. His eyes drifted across my face for a moment, before landing on my lips. "Why did you say kissing was a hard no?"

I bit my lip, not sure I wanted to admit the reason I said I didn't want to kiss him. It'd fuel his 'we should be a couple' fire. Though at this point, I'd be lying to myself if I said I wasn't going to admit I wanted him when he pulled his whole stupid leave me alone for a few hours to see how I feel thing.

"I wasn't … it would make things complicated."

"I want things more complicated."

Stupid, rude, stupid man.

I let go of his shirt and tangled my finger into his hair, pulling his face to mine and pressing our lips together. His lips were so soft and he tasted like me. And this time, when I thought of him being mine, I thought of him relaxing on the couch, patting the cushion next to him, and pulling me into his lap when I sat down. I pictured him sleeping beside me in bed while I binged a new show. I pictured him cooking for me and reminding me to eat when I got caught up with work.

Matt started thrusting with his grinds, banging the table into the wall so hard that there were probably going to be marks on the wall. If I pointed them out, Matt would fix them.

Another thrust and I broke apart. It was soft, warmth spreading through me and tensing my body, making me shake. I wanted him to get this feeling too.

"Thatta girl." Matt loosened his hold on me, hands falling to my hips, tightening before one more thrust brought him to his own oblivion. I paid attention to the way his hips shook, the way his fingers dug into me, the way his lips quivered. It was beautiful. He was beautiful when he came.

Our heavy breaths mingled, hot and muggy when we pulled our lips apart. We stayed like that, holding each other for a moment longer. Somehow, we both started rubbing circles into each other's skin with our thumbs. The rhythm matched our slowing breaths. And when our breaths started evening out, Matt said, "I'm gonna go now. Okay, Kas?"

I blinked. Nodded. Nodded again as the words started to process. Right, Matt was leaving for the day. Along with his stupid plan of making me confess how I felt, he probably had moving stuff to handle.

Matt pulled away from me, walking off to the bathroom. When he returned, his pants were back on. He bent down in front of me and grabbed my clothes, slipping them up my legs. I slid off the table and Matt pulled my pants the rest of the way up.

"I know you're stubborn, so I won't expect you to text me asking me to come back early. But I think you're gonna miss me."

"Cocky bastard," I murmured and Matt smiled, a big smile that showed off his dimples.

"I'll miss you too." Matt took my hand, kissing the back of it, squeezing it before letting go. Then he left.

Stupid, rude man making me feel things.

* * *

I'd switched between seven different shows, unable to

focus on any of them for more than fifteen minutes. Even the spy family anime, which I'd genuinely been excited about even if I used it as an excuse before.

And when I switched to cleaning to distract myself, all Matt's shit kept getting in the way. Headphones on the coffee table, hoodies draped over the back of the couch, even a sock stuck between the cushions. One sock, no pair.

Frustrated, I piled all his crap together and went to his room to dump it. Went to *my* guest room. But when I stood in the open door, his things clutched tightly in my arms, I just … gave up. I dropped all his shit on the floor and crawled into his bed. Everything smelled like him. His stupid smell that made my mouth a little watery, but also made me comfortable.

Stupid Matt was gonna make me ask him to stay. And then we'd spend all our time being a stupid couple, blessedly without the awkward first dates. And whenever he came back from the gym, arms sweaty, I'd be able to just call him to bed. He was right and everything would work out and it was frustrating.

"Whatcha doing in my bed, Kas?"

I jerked up, Matt's comfort pooling around my waist. Huh, guess I fell asleep. Well, whatever, I didn't want to talk to Matt's stupid face right now. I was mad at him for doing all this shit, wanting us to be together right when he was moving out. So, I plopped back down on the bed and pulled up the covers. It felt stupid for my boyfriend to move out as soon as we got together.

The bed sank as Matt sat beside me. I turned the other way. Matt leaned across me, pinning me between his arm and body. So, I turned onto my stomach, which wasn't really comfortable since the blankets had started to get twisted.

"Kas, what're you doing?" There was a laugh in his voice. I bet he was smiling. Stupid, bad timing man.

"I'm enjoying my soon-to-be vacated guest room."

"Uh-huh. It looks to me like you climbed in here because you missed me. Does that mean you want me too?"

"You know I do, stupid."

Matt leaned forward, his body pressing into me. "I'm sorry, what was that?"

"You're stupid."

"Kas, if you don't come out of the blankets, I'm gonna have to tickle you."

I rolled over and pushed the blankets down. "I don't want you to move."

Matt's smile fell to shock.

"I mean, it's stupid. If you want to date, what would be the point of moving? I know technically, that's a big step in a relationship, but seeing each other less seems like a step backwards. And we already know we can live together, so that's not a problem. Except for your shoes, you really should be able to put them in the cubby."

"Kas?"

"And I'm not saying you should start sleeping in my room. So, you'll still have your own space. And you already said the only thing that's really changing is the fucking. And –"

"Kas?"

"What?"

"I have a few conditions for me to stay?"

My brow furrowed. "What?"

"One, you've got to let me pay rent or something."

"But I'm not paying rent."

"You're paying your mortgage, that's the same thing. Let me pay half."

I considered talking him down to a quarter, but I could use the extra money to buy him a better knife set. He liked to cook and the knives I had were functional but not what I imagined someone who actually cooked would pick out.

"Fine."

"Good. Condition two, I wanna try and watch that spy show with you. Just to see."

God, this man. So fucking stubborn and adorable.

"Fine."

"And last one. I get to kiss you."

"You're not going to let that go, are you?"

"Never. So, what do you say?"

"It wasn't a real hard no, I just ... didn't want to kiss you if you were gonna leave."

"So, since I'm not leaving ..." he trailed off. And solely because I was tired of this conversation, I pulled him in for a kiss.

EPILOGUE

Matt

I rubbed my hands together, taking in the, if I do say so myself, exquisite meal I'd made. Creamy risotto topped with scallops, bacon, and chives. It was perfect, Kasey was gonna love it. Hopefully, she loved it so much that she'd be receptive when I told her I loved her.

I ran both hands through my hair, letting out a long breath. It'd only been three months since I didn't move out. That felt like it was too soon. But also, in the past three months, I'd spent as many nights in her bed as I would have gone on dates with another woman. And those nights were never about sex. Well, there was plenty of sex, but also just cuddling while she worked or watched a show.

"Hey Matt," Kasey called as she walked through the front door. I took a deep breath and hurried to set the table before she rounded the hall. It looked good. This should go well. She'll definitely say it back. Or at least not give me shit for saying it too soon. Or not just stare blankly at me, that'd be the worst.

Kasey came into a room, a soft smile lighting her face as she took in the prepared meal. "Shit, this looks really good. Thanks, Matt. Love you."

Kasey kissed me on the cheek, then took her spot at the table. God, I loved that she just kissed me now. I still wasn't used to it. I hadn't expected her to be so affectionate. But she took nearly every opportunity to touch me, even if it was just sitting beside me on the couch just close enough that our thighs touched. And ...

"Wait a second, did you just say you loved me?"

Kasey raised her head, a spoon full of food halfway to her mouth. "Yeah, why?"

Oh my god, this woman.

"Kaaaaaassssseyyyy." I dragged a hand over my face and then pulled her up, crushing her to me.

"What'd I do?" she asked, looking down at the abandoned food.

"I had a whole thing set up here."

She looked back up at me, then to the food, then at me. Her cheeks slowly took on a pink tint as her mouth dropped. "Oh. Sorry."

"I made a nice meal for us, curated the perfect playlist, and you stole my thunder."

"Sorry," she said through a giggle. "I just ... well I just said it without really thinking."

I rested my head on her forehead and sighed. "Yeah, well I guess I'm the more romantic one of the two of us."

She hummed in response, her hands toying with the hem of my shirt. I let her wait, not saying anything until she spoke. Just a little payback for ruining my set up.

"So, are you gonna say it back or not?"

"Say what?"

Kasey sighed and turned out of my arms, moving to sit back down. I grabbed her wrist and pulled her back to me. "Come on Kas, you know I love you."

I kissed her and she hummed her approval, wrapping her arms around my neck and pulling herself up so her legs could go around my waist. And that's when I knew our food was gonna go cold tonight. Again.

ABOUT THE AUTHOR

K.E. Monteith is an adult romance writer living in Northern Virginia with her two rambunctious dogs and partner. Her debut novella, ALL GROWN UP, is a gender-swapped brother's best friend romance released in February 2022. And her upcoming novella, QUITTING MY BOSS, is an office romance coming out in December 2022.

BOOKS BY THIS AUTHOR

All Grown Up

In this gender-swapped brother's best friends, Kaleb has been in love with Lexi Jacobs for as long as he could remember. And even ten years later, he's still holding a flame for her. But now that Lexi is in town, staying at his childhood home for his brother's wedding, he can prove that he's not a little kid anymore

When Lexi sees Kaleb Russel for the first time in ten years, she is stunned by how he grew up. He was barely 14 when she left and now ... he wasn't. But this wasn't the time or place. She was here for her best friend's wedding, to be his best man and plan his bachelor party, not get the hots for his kid brother. But that get's harder and harder when Kaleb pins her to a wall and asks if she still sees him as a kid.

Third Time's The Charm

LUCY SHEPPARD

Ten years ago Jake kissed me and ran. Eight years ago I learned the reason why. Five years ago, Jake came back for a night and I let him have what we both wanted, knowing he wouldn't be able to stay in town after all he went through.

But that night led to a kid. And while I wouldn't take it back for the world, now that Jake's made a surprise visit and finds out he's a dad, I can't let my love for him sway me anymore.

JAKE WHEATLEY

Ten years ago I stole Lucy's first kiss because I thought it'd be the only thing I could have from her. Five years ago I took something even more important. And now I found out that night led to a kid. Lucy and my kid.

I can't be a father, not when mine was the way he was. But I can't bring myself to leave Lucy's side this time. Maybe if it's just a little, I won't turn out like him.

Third Time's the Charm is a standalone, steamy romance. This novella does contain material triggering for some: sexually explicit content, depictions of parental abuse, neglect, and demotic violence, and a depiction of panic attacks.

UPCOMING RELEASE

CONTINUE READING FOR A PREVIEW OF

Quitting my Boss

K.E. MONTEITH

PREVIEW OF
QUITTING MY BOSS

Mr. Mogan Bleckard, CEO of the largest chain bookstore in the Northeast, has the hots for me. At least I was pretty certain. But there was, of course, the nagging doubt that there was no way in hell Mr. Bleckard, hottest bachelor in any city he stood in, would actually want to fuck his secretary. It was too stereotypical, too book trope-y to be real. Except there was no denying how he looked at me, eyes hungry, breath labored. How could I not think he wanted to jump into my pants? I certainly wanted to. Yesterday he tossed a crumpled sheet of paper over my shoulder to the trash by his door and when he missed, asked me to pick it up on my way out. Was it a dumb and mildly childish way to get me to bend over? Yes. But did I enjoy having his eyes glued to my ass? Also yes.

But I knew nothing about Mr. Bleckard as a person. I mean, I know how he takes his coffee, his typical order at his five favorite restaurants, and how much time he spent at the gym every week. And that was after only a month of working here. But that wasn't enough to really know him, nothing worth starting a relationship on. Sex though …

"Rachel." Mr. Bleckard's voice came from behind me, sharp and ice cold. I turned to see the tall suited man staring at me from where he leaned on his door frame, light green eyes grazing over me. Goosebumps. This man gave me goosebumps every time he looked at me. It wouldn't be a problem if he'd just look at me normally, if he kept the lust out of his eyes for just a minute. It made it hard to work sometimes.

"Yes, sir?" I asked, trying to catch a glimpse of his calendar out of the corner of my eyes. It was Tuesday and he normally didn't have anything scheduled for Tuesday. He said that he kept Monday free to deal with problems that arose over the weekends and Tuesday free to catch up on any work missed on Monday. It was as logical as any other reason I guess. But if he didn't have a meeting scheduled, he shouldn't be needing me until after lunch when managers submitted their reports.

Mr. Bleckard didn't say anything. Instead, he went into his office, leaving the door open. I took my cue and followed him inside. His office was sharply modern. No personality, no pictures, no colorful pens. Just black and glass. If he laid me out on that desk it'd be cold. A nice sharp sensation in contrast to the heat of our bodies.

I stayed near the door as I waited for his instructions. Mr. Bleckard was sitting on the edge of his desk, the one I *wasn't* having certain thoughts about. He looked me over again and stood, walking up to me so close that our bodies were just an inch apart. He reached over my shoulder and kept walking. I stepped back until my ass hit the door, slamming it closed. One hand rested against the door, the other reached up and took my chin.

My mind went blank. Not a single thought could enter my brain. Every single one of my brain cells was hyper-focused on Mr. Bleckard's touch and the heat it brought.

"There's nothing on the calendar for today, right?"

"No, sir." I don't know how I managed words with his mouth so close to mine.

"I want you, badly." He pushed against me, the hard bulge in his pants making my mouth water.

"Yes." He hadn't really asked a question. But as soon as that word of permission was out of my mouth, his lips were on me. He didn't start with my mouth, he started at my neck, small kisses turning into long licks up to my earlobe. He nibbled that tender flesh and I squeaked, embarrassing myself. I covered my mouth and Mr. Bleckard pulled back, eyes narrowing at me.

"This office is soundproof, Rachel." He pulled my hand away and this time he took my lips with force, immediately opening up to search for my tongue. And I let him, met his tongue with mine and relished the sensation, a moan escaping the back of my throat. Mr. Bleckard smirked against my lips. "I want to hear every single one of your sounds. Don't hold back."

He grabbed my ass, pulling and lifting me up so that my center rested against his hardness. Instinctively, my legs wrapped around him, my skirt riding up my thighs.

Mr. Bleckard pressed me up against the door, hands dropping to lift my skirt the rest of the way, gripping me with as much need as I felt.

"These skirts have been driving me fucking insane, Rachel." Duly noted. I'll get them in every color and pattern available. Bleckard's hands slipped under my panties and squeezed, rocking me against his cock. And just as my eyes started to roll back into my head, he grumbled, "Don't wear them on Mondays. I need to get work done, for fucks sake."

Guess I don't need to buy more skirts after all.

His hands moved again, this time to my shirt, undoing the buttons painfully slow. Bleckard must have thought the same because instead of undoing the next button, he tore the shirt completely off, the remaining buttons flying off. "I'll buy you a new one."

I couldn't even bring myself to care, because as soon as the shirt was parted, his hands slid up my tank top and under my bra, he pinched my nipples ruthlessly. The sharp sensation had me moaning, rocking harder against his cock. Bleckard smirked and returned his lips to my neck, sucking just under my ear where I'd put perfume on this morning.

"Morgan," I moan. His hands and lips stilled. I waited breathlessly for him to pull away. The fog of lust told me I could say his name. Even if this was just sex, that should be okay, right?

"You can't do that to me, Rachel." He thrust into me, rough and relieving. "Understand?"

"Yes, sir." That shouldn't have been my answer. I should've stopped right there. If a man wasn't going to let me scream his name during sex, then I shouldn't be having sex with him. But I wanted it so bad. And his fingers had moved to undo his pants. And once he was free, he was pushing aside my panties. And ...

"So fucking wet for me."

"Yes, sir." And I was a goner from then on.

Made in the USA
Las Vegas, NV
23 August 2022

53779897R00056